Shepherding Sam

by

Melinda Johnson

ANCIENT FAITH PUBLISHING
Chesterton, Indiana

Shepherding Sam
Text copyright © 2016 Melinda Johnson
Cover and interior illustrations by Clare Freeman

Published by:
    Ancient Faith Publishing
    A division of Ancient Faith Ministries
    PO Box 748
    Chesterton IN 46304

978-1-944967-07-9

PRINTED IN THE UNITED STATES OF AMERICA

25 24 23 22 21 20 19   16 15 14 13 12 11 10 9 8 7 6 5 4 3 2

For Majesta,
who said there should be a corgi in the book.

For the real "Aunt Eva" and her husband Rick,
with thanks for the lively and wonderful Sunday school home
they create for the children at our parish.

For the real "Elias" and his brothers,
who constantly remind me why boys are awesome.

For Sharon, with love and thanks
for her company on the journey.

CHAPTER

ONE

SAUCER THE CORGI came to the monastery on a rainy day. Each time a raindrop fell on his pointed ears, he bounced into the air and shook his head so hard his ears flopped like windshield wipers.

Saucer came from a nearby farm where sheep were once kept. His parents and grandparents and great-grandparents were all sheepherding dogs. But now the farmer was old, and his children had moved away. He could no longer keep the new litters of puppies, with no more sheep to herd.

Saucer didn't mind. He was too young and frisky to be sad for long, and he was a hopeful puppy. Every morning, when Saucer woke up, he rolled onto his back, waggled his paws in the air, yawned so hard that he lolloped over sideways, and jumped up full of hope. "Arf! Arf!" said Saucer to the world. "Arf!" *Today, I will finally be a herding dog.*

The farmer brought Saucer to the monastery gate and handed him over to Sister Katherine, who took care of the nuns' small animal farm.

"Goodbye, little feller," said the farmer. His gnarled hand rested on Saucer's furry head.

"Arf!" said Saucer, licking the farmer's hand.

"Hello, Saucer," said Sister Katherine. Saucer licked her hand, too. She set him down on the grass and watched him frolic with the raindrops. Sister Katherine smiled.

Just then the refectory door opened, and a group of nuns came out. The nuns all wore long black robes and black head coverings. They were all smiling, all moving together in a group.

Saucer bounded across the wet grass, barking joyfully. He raced around the nuns, nipping their ankles and the flapping hems of their gowns, butting their legs with his head, urging them to follow his lead.

"Lord, have mercy," cried Sister Katherine. "He thinks the sisters are sheep!"

The nuns began to laugh, and the soft chorus of voices sounded like "Baaaaha, baaaaha." Saucer took a bite of the lead nun's black robe and pulled

hard, looking up at her face and waggling his ears encouragingly.

"Oh, dear," said Sister Katherine to herself. "Sisters!" she called. "Can you step away from each other and stop baa—I mean, could you keep quiet for a minute? Saucer is confused."

The nuns tried to stop laughing. Sister Anna stepped away from the group.

"Arf!" Saucer raced between the nuns and pounced on Sister Anna's feet.

"Here, Saucer, here!" Sister Katherine chirped loudly and clapped her hands.

Sister Anna shook her head. "We better just stand here and pray."

It took several minutes to convince Saucer that the sisters weren't sheep. Even when Sister Katherine picked him up and patted his back in a soothing way, Saucer's face said plainly that he wasn't convinced.

"Those are nuns, little corgi. Nuns. Not sheep."

They look like sheep to me, said Saucer's face. He barked one more time, having the last word.

"Come and see your house, Saucer," suggested Sister Katherine.

Saucer gazed up into her face. Sister Katherine was tall, with long fingers and long feet, and God had made her face in a smiling shape. Saucer also had a smiling face. (Most corgis do.) He reached up to lick Sister Katherine's chin, and he grinned at her as she carried him down the path to the animal farm.

There is only one path at the monastery. It runs along to the door of every building and the edge of every garden. Sometimes, the path seems to travel in circles, but there are no breaks in the path and no dead ends. You need only stay on it and keep walking to reach the place where you need to be.

The path starts and ends at the church door. It winds down a gentle hill, curves around the tidy rows of vegetables sprouting in the garden, and swerves over to the parking lot. Coming back into the monastery, it rolls around the apple orchard and passes a wooden fence with a squeaky gate, on its way to the nuns' quarters.

The animals live inside this wooden fence, and whenever someone opens the squeaky gate, every animal welcomes the visitor. It sounds like this: Squeeeak ... click. "Baaaa! Baaaaaa! Quack! Quack! Hee-haw!

Buk-buk! Woof!!"

Sister Katherine opened the squeaky gate every morning after prayers, and she opened it now, with Saucer tucked under her arm. "Here are your new friends, Saucer. In just a minute, you'll hear them all singing a welcome to you!"

Squeeeak . . . click.

"Baaaa! Baaaaaa! Quack! Quack! Hee-haw! Buk-buk! Woof!"

Sister Katherine shook her head, smiling. "Good morning! God bless you!" she said, patting the eager animals who thrust their heads through the hutch doors and fence slats around her.

Saucer's head turned in so many directions that

he almost flipped out of Sister Katherine's arms. "Arf! Arf! Arf-arf-arf!" Saucer couldn't bark fast enough for all the things he wanted to say.

Sister Katherine set Saucer down in front of a square red doghouse, a few feet inside the farmyard gate. Saucer sniffed it all over with his pointed nose, wagged his stumpy tail, and let his tongue loll out of his grinning mouth. Two seconds later, he was out of the doghouse and prancing through the animal farm, inspecting all the pens. There might not be any nuns in those pens, but there were other animals, and Saucer thought they had herding possibilities.

On most farms, animals live with their own kind, but at the monastery, the animals lived with their own friends. The first pen Saucer came to was home to a black-and-white border collie and a golden Araucana

chicken. Aero the Guard Dog and Butterscotch the
Guard Chicken had come to the monastery together and
refused to be separated. They spent all day in opposite
corners of their pen, staring hard at the other animals
and reporting to each other over their shoulders. "Buk-
buk! Woof, woof!" Every few minutes, they raced across
the pen, switching corners.

Two gray bunnies lived next door to Aero and
Butterscotch. Someone named them Mary and Martha,
like the sisters in the Gospels, but as they grew up, it
became clear that both bunnies were misnamed. Martha
spent her days cuddled peacefully in the sunniest corner
of the pen, basking in the warmth and light. Mary scampered around the pen from morning to night, rearrang-
ing bits of straw and knocking over the food bowl just
for the satisfaction of picking it up again.

A family of goats enjoyed the large corner pen. Their names were Hop, Skip, Jump, Et Cetera, and So Forth, and they were the noisiest members of the farm family. There was plenty of room to hop, skip, and jump in their roomy pen, but what they loved best was sticking their heads through the fence and commenting loudly on whatever the nuns were doing. So Forth stood lookout at the corner of the pen. Whenever she saw a nun, she sounded the alarm. "Baaaaaaaaaaaaa!" Her family ran to see what the nun was doing, and all five of them frolicked around the fence corner, bleating excitedly until the nun disappeared from view.

Bethlehem the donkey thought the goats were amazing. He didn't understand them, but he loved to watch the goats as much as the goats loved to watch the nuns. On his other side were the ducks, and they were interesting, too. Most days, Bethlehem trotted from the goat side to the duck side, waiting for his mysterious friends to do something entertaining. He was a small, quiet donkey with soft gray hair and long ears that twitched around, listening to the sounds of the world. He only brayed when he was nervous or when he thought the goats were funny.

The duck pen was built around a small pond with a pebbly beach and fluffy grasses growing at the edges for nesting. Dickens was the largest duck, with a shining green head and tweedy brown feathers. The others (in order of size) were Shakespeare, Charlotte, Emily, Cuthbert, Ignatius, Kassiani, Photios, Moses, and Daniel. The ducks followed each other around the pen. Whenever he wanted a change, Dickens quacked like a chairman making a motion. Charlotte and Emily seconded the motion—"Quack, quack!"— and Shakespeare rounded up the ducklings and shooed them along, following Dickens wherever the committee had decided to go.

Saucer spent his first afternoon galloping up and down the farm path between the pens. His eyes darted back and forth, from the goats to the ducks, from the donkey to the bunnies. His nose waggled in the air. Every inch of his little furry body was springing with joy and purpose. His herd! He had found it!

It took Saucer a full day to realize the problem with his herd.

His herd was stuck. The animals lived in separate pens, and they never came out all at once, in a group, so he could round them up and nip their ankles and bring them safely home.

Saucer was disappointed, but he didn't despair. Saucer was always hopeful.

Every morning, when Sister Katherine came to the animal farm, she found Saucer on patrol, trotting up and down the little path between the rows of pens. He would come to greet her, and she would let him out for a run in the grassy space beyond the farm. But Saucer would stay outside only for a short time. He wanted to get back to his herd.

The nuns tried to distract him. They took him for long walks. They brought him toys that squeaked and jingled. They threw sticks and tried to teach him to fetch. Saucer grinned at them, offered to round them up (in case they had changed their minds), then trotted back to the animal farm to keep watch over his herd. *Someday,* Saucer told himself, *somehow.*

"He'll be happier when the children come to visit," said Sister Katherine to Sister Anna, watching Saucer marching up and down along the row of pens. "Puppies and children always enjoy each other."

"Do you think he will try to herd the children?" asked Sister Anna. "Are you sure we can let him play with the little ones?"

"Maybe not the very smallest children, but the older children wouldn't mind."

"There doesn't seem to be any purpose in it," said Sister Anna, after a moment. "I wish we could train him to use that energy for something else."

"It's all those generations of sheepherding ancestors," replied Sister Katherine. "He hasn't learned yet that it's not his job."

"That doesn't seem fair to him. I wonder why God has kept that instinct so strong when Saucer can't use it anymore."

"It's a mystery," said Sister Katherine. But she wondered about it for the rest of the day.

C H A P T E R

TWO

A WEEK AFTER SAUCER came to the monastery, Sister Katherine brought a friend with her when she came to let him out for his daily walk. Saucer saw them coming across the grassy space toward the animal farm. He stuck his nose through the fence and sniffed, curious.

Sister Katherine reached down to pat Saucer's head as soon as he came through the gate.

"Saucer, this is Aunt Eva. She's visiting us today."

Aunt Eva gave Saucer her hand to sniff, then

scratched that unreachable spot behind his ears. Saucer wiggled blissfully and pawed her shoe. The ladies started walking, and Saucer frisked around them, enjoying the grass but stopping now and then to stare at Aunt Eva and listen to her voice. Aunt Eva wore glasses. They sparkled in the sunshine, and her eyes sparkled behind them.

"I'd like to bring the kids again, probably on Friday, but I wanted to let you know that I'll have Sam with me this time," Aunt Eva was saying to Sister Katherine.

"We love having the children here, and you know we aren't worried about Sam," said Sister Katherine, taking her eyes off Saucer for a moment to look at her friend.

"I know you aren't, and I'm thankful for that. I

just wanted to touch base with you before he comes so we can think about how to help him while he's visiting."

"What works best for him?" asked Sister Katherine. "How do his parents like you to handle things?"

Aunt Eva sighed. "My brother and his wife are good people, and they love Sam very much, but we all agree that we really haven't found what works best for him yet. Third grade has been hard all year, and we haven't even gotten him in the door at church. He's like a little tornado. Everywhere he goes, there's a ruckus."

Saucer bounded back to the ladies and sat down right in front of them. They stopped walking just in time to keep from tripping over him. Sister Katherine stooped and patted Saucer absent-mindedly. Saucer stared up at Aunt Eva. Aunt Eva stared back.

"I wonder if he likes dogs," mused Aunt Eva. "Do you like boys, Saucer?"

"Arf!" said Saucer.

Sister Katherine chuckled. "Saucer likes every living creature he's seen, and I've never met a boy who didn't like dogs. But I should warn you. Saucer hasn't managed to overcome his sheepherding instincts."

Aunt Eva laughed out loud. "The puppy who wants to lead and the boy who refuses to follow. What a pair they'll be!"

"Lord have mercy on Saucer and Sam," said Sister Katherine, crossing herself.

Saucer and Sam, said Saucer to himself. *Who is Sam?*

Aunt Eva and Sister Katherine hugged each other. They walked Saucer back to his doghouse and gave him a cookie. Saucer flopped down next to his water bowl and chewed on the cookie. He watched Aunt Eva and Sister Katherine walk away across the grass.

Sam, thought Saucer again, nudging the stub end of his cookie. *Saucer and Sam.*

CHAPTER

THREE

UNLIKE SAUCER THE CORGI, Sam the Boy came to the monastery for the first time on a sunny day. Spring flowers bloomed in the gardens, birds sang in the trees, and Sam was so mad that he kicked all four tires of Aunt Eva's minivan before it ever left the driveway.

Aunt Eva took no notice. She stood by the sliding door of the van, waiting for Sam to stop kicking tires. When he ran out of tires, he climbed into his seat as slowly as possible. Aunt Eva told all the cousins to buckle their seatbelts, took her place at the wheel, and drove off down the road.

Unlike most of Sam's relatives and friends, Aunt Eva did not worry about taking Sam to the monastery. Aunt Eva believed in patience and the power of love, and tire-kicking didn't scare her. Neither did anything else.

Sam looked out the window and made horrible faces at passing cars all the way there. It was a lot of faces for a lot of cars. He didn't have time to notice anything else, such as a hamster in his pocket.

Sam had no idea Piggybear had come with him until Sister Anna started talking about prayers. He was sitting with his cousins and their friends on a wooden bench in the grassy space near the animal farm. Aunt Eva had settled them there with Sister Anna and a snack while she visited the abbess, but Sam didn't want his crackers, and he was tired of waiting on the bench.

Saucer was sitting under the bench, doing his best to obey Sister Katherine's morning instructions. "When our friends come today, I want you to remember something, Saucer," she had said. "I want you to remember they are people, not sheep."

Saucer loved Sister Katherine and wanted to make her happy. So he sat under the bench, watching the children's shoes swinging and scuffling in front of him. *People are not sheep,* Saucer told himself. But once or twice, he nibbled the back of Sam's pant leg. Something about that boy smelled extra interesting to him.

Sam had his raincoat on because his mother thought it might rain. In the bright spring sunshine, it felt hot and itchy. Sam unzipped it halfway. Sister Anna looked like she might be about to pray, but he had been thinking about his annoying raincoat, so he had no idea what was going on.

Sam nudged his cousin Macrina, who was next to him on the bench. "What are we talking about?" he whispered.

"Do you ever pay attention?" Macrina whispered back.

Sam rolled his eyes. Saucer snuffled at his shoe. Sam pulled his legs up so he could sit cross-legged on the bench. Saucer sank down in the grass and rested his nose on his paws.

Sister Anna turned her head and smiled at Sam wiggling on the bench.

"Nuns pray all the time," said Sister Anna. "Your cousin Matthew wanted to know what nuns pray about."

"Yeah," said Elias, Matthew's brother. "Because what could you pray about that would last all day?"

Sam thought Elias had a point.

"What do you think?" asked Sister Anna. "If you were a nun, what would you be praying about?"

"To save the world?" asked Macrina, who always made the grown-ups proud.

"There's no way I'd ever be a nun," said Sam, and he was about to poke Macrina for being such a show-off when suddenly, he had a strange feeling. Something about it felt familiar, but he couldn't think what it was.

Under the bench, Saucer wiggled closer to Sam, snuffing loudly.

Sam started to poke Macrina a second time, and the feeling happened again. Sam looked around.

Macrina was gazing at Sister Anna, hanging on every word she said. The rest of Sam's cousins and friends were kicking each other's feet under the bench.

The feeling came again—a feathery, tickly feeling close to where his coat pocket lay on his lap. Sam opened his mouth to ask Macrina if anything was crawling on him, but the words never came. The feeling skittered up the inside of Sam's coat, snuffled around his neck, and scampered up his ear onto his head.

"Piggybear!" yelled Sam, clutching the air around his head. "What are you doing here?"

Elias, Macrina, and seven other children swiveled around on the bench. Saucer backed out from under the bench and started barking excitedly.

"There's a hamster on your head," screamed Macrina, and she fell backward off the bench onto the grass. Sister Anna rushed to help her. Saucer rushed to help Sister Anna. Sam clambered up on the bench to get away from all the other children, who suddenly surged toward him.

"It's so cute!" said nine different children at once. "Can I pat it? Can I hold it?"

"Help!" cried Sam. He cupped his hands over Piggybear, whose tiny pink toes were tangled in Sam's hair. "She's going to jump off my head. Nun lady, you got to help me. Help! Help!"

"Don't let her fall, or the dog will eat her," called Macrina, flat on her back in the grass but still giving directions.

"No, he won't," said Matthew.

"That's stupid," said Elias. "Dogs don't eat hamsters."

"You don't know if dogs eat hamsters or not, Elias, and don't call me stupid!" said Macrina, scrambling to her feet with Sister Anna's help.

"I know Saucer wouldn't eat a hamster," replied Elias. "And he's the only dog here."

Macrina sniffed.

Sister Anna came over to Sam. "Can you lift her very carefully and put her back into your pocket?"

"She's grabbing my hair. You can't pull on a hamster. Hamsters have fingers!"

"I'll help you. We can be very gentle. Children, please try to be quiet."

Saucer barked. The children stopped shouting. Saucer nudged a few of them toward the bench.

Carefully, Sister Anna folded her hands around Sam's hands and began lifting Piggybear. She pulled gently, and Piggybear's tiny fingers uncurled from Sam's hair. Sam brought the hamster down off his head and cuddled her soft little body against his chest with a gasp of relief. Piggybear nibbled the shiny zipper on Sam's raincoat. Her bright eyes gleamed up at Sam. Her whiskers flickered.

"How did your hamster get here?" asked Elias,

who wanted to know the reason for everything in life.

"I don't know," said Sam. "She got out of her cage, I guess."

"Are you sure that dog isn't going to eat the hamster?" asked Macrina, picking grass off her clothes.

Saucer snorted and tossed his head.

"Saucer doesn't like you," said Matthew, and he sat down on the grass to pat the corgi.

"Come to the kitchen," said Sister Anna. "It's almost time for lunch, and we can find a box there for your hamster to ride in until you can bring her safely home."

"You could feed her at lunch," said Elias. "I bet she would like monastery food."

"Saucer likes monastery food, too," said Matthew. "Can Saucer come to lunch?"

"Boys, why don't you take Saucer to his dog-house?" suggested Sister Anna. "He has food there, and you can refill his water dish from the spigot by the gate."

Elias and Matthew raced off. Saucer's head went back and forth, watching the running boys, turning back to Sam and his hamster.

"Saucer! Come on, Saucer!" called Elias, running backward and clapping his hands to get the puppy's attention.

"Arf!" said Saucer. With a last glance at Sam, Saucer scampered after Elias and Matthew, chasing the boys and their flying feet.

The rest of the children followed Sister Anna to

the refectory. Sam was careful to stay near Sister Anna, who had promised him a box for Piggybear, and Macrina was careful to stay away from Sam, who couldn't even sit on a bench without getting in trouble. All three were thankful that Sam and his hamster would be going home soon.

"Well?" said Sister Katherine, as she and Aunt Eva walked the children back to the parking lot after lunch.

"Better luck next time," said Aunt Eva confidently. "Even God didn't create the world in one day."

C H A P T E R

FOUR

SAUCER SLEPT half in and half out of his dog-house. Sometimes his front end was in the doghouse and his back end was outside, and sometimes the other way around.

The morning after Sam's visit, Saucer woke up early. He rolled onto his back, waggled his paws in the air, yawned so hard that he lolloped over sideways, and jumped up full of hope. "Arf! Arf!" said Saucer to the world. "Arf!" *Today, I will finally be a herding dog.*

Across the path from Saucer's doghouse, Aero

and Butterscotch were also awake. Before she came to the monastery, Butterscotch had lived on a farm with a very loud rooster. He woke the whole farm before the sun finished rising, and Butterscotch could still hear him in her dreams.

"Woof!" said Aero, stretching out his front paws and waggling his tail section high in the air.

Saucer trotted over to the chicken pen fence. He watched Aero and Butterscotch having breakfast and taking up their favorite positions in opposite corners of the pen. Aero was on Saucer's side of the pen. The two dogs sniffed each other's noses.

Why do you stay in there? Saucer asked Aero.

Because Butterscotch belongs to me. I stay here to take care of her.

Saucer nodded understandingly. Butterscotch was Aero's herd.

I met a boy yesterday, Saucer told Aero. *He was called Sam.*

Was it a nice boy? Some boys are good to play with. Aero's ears twitched. His eyes were black like Saucer's.

Saucer thought about Sam. There seemed to be a lot of noise around Sam and people flapping their arms and shaking their heads.

I don't think Sam knows what to do, Saucer decided. *He doesn't do things that other people do. He doesn't fit in with his herd.*

Aero reared up and put his front paws on the top of his fence. *Some people don't understand about herds.*

Saucer wasn't sure about that.

Aero dropped down again on all four paws. *People don't know they are part of a herd. They think herding is just for animals.*

Saucer scratched his ear with his back paw. *I could help. I could show them. But Sister Katherine keeps saying, "People aren't sheep, Saucer."*

I just look after Butterscotch, that's what I do. And Aero trotted off to switch places with his chicken partner.

Saucer stretched and wiggled. *Who is my Butterscotch?* he wondered. *How can I get to this herd with so many fences?*

Saucer lapped up some water from his bowl and went to wait for Sister Katherine by the gate.

CHAPTER FOUR

He thought about Sam again. *I wonder. Will he come back?*

C H A P T E R

FIVE

AUNT EVA CHECKED Piggybear's cage herself before she brought Sam to the monastery the second time. Piggybear sat up on her haunches and washed her pink nose with her tiny pink fingers. "Yes," said Aunt Eva, "you're very cute, and here's a sunflower seed for you. But you aren't coming with us today!"

Sam made horrible faces at passing cars all the way to the monastery. It was an afternoon in late spring. His cousins chattered excitedly because the whole parish was coming this time for a picnic. It was Bright Monday, the day after Pascha.

Sam crossed his eyes and stuck his tongue out at three more cars, but his face was getting tired. He rested his head against the glass.

All the cousins tumbled out of the minivan the minute it stopped moving. The monastery parking lot was full of people and voices. Sam's cousins disappeared into the crowd.

"Come along, Sam," said Aunt Eva. She patted his head. Sam ducked away from her and walked along the path, scuffing the toes of his shoes.

When Sam reached the picnic area, Elias and Matthew were tending the campfire with their friends from church, and Macrina was sitting on a nearby rock with a little girl with wild red curls.

"Did you know if you poke the fire, it will make it burn more?" Elias demonstrated, using a large stick he'd found under the pine trees.

Matthew nodded. "We're Boy Scouts. We could make this fire burn whatever way we want."

"Are you two going to start up again already?" Macrina rolled her eyes.

"Only if you're going to boss us around," Elias said. He and Matthew looked at each other and grinned.

Around them, parents and nuns unpacked baskets of food and spread blankets on the grass under the trees. Singing broke out here and there. "Christ is Risen from the dead, trampling down death by death . . . " The fire sparked and crackled. A breeze rustled the leaves of tall trees standing around the picnic ground.

Sam stuffed his hands in his pockets. Aunt Eva was talking to three of her friends. He edged away from the group by the campfire.

"Sam?" He heard Aunt Eva's voice calling him. It just proved what he secretly believed: Aunt Eva had eyes in the back of her head, and probably on both sides of it, too.

Sam kicked four pebbles off the path as hard as he could. But he came back to the campfire because Aunt Eva would hunt him down if he didn't.

Four children sat on rocks around the fire: his cousin Macrina sat next to the little girl, and Elias and

Matthew sat across from each other, poking the fire with long sticks.

"Tell a story, M'crina," said the little girl, cupping her two hands carefully to protect a tiny friend. "Me and this ladybug want to hear it."

Macrina flipped her braid over her shoulder. "What kind of story, Brigid?"

"All the kinds of story."

Elias looked up. "Can we help? We could put in awesome stuff. A dragon or something."

"Yeah!! A *dragon!*" Matthew waved his stick in the air. "Let's make it happen at a monastery like this one."

"Yeah!" The boys jumped onto their rocks and shook their sticks in the air like swords.

"Only if the dragon doesn't bite, okay?" Brigid let her ladybug escape. She slid along the rock toward Macrina.

"*Duh*," said Sam, coming a little closer. "How could a fake dragon bite you?"

Macrina stared at Sam as if he had crawled out from under a rotten log.

"We would poke the dragon in the eye with our sticks," said Matthew. "But don't worry, Brigid, because if imaginary teeth bite you, you don't feel anything."

"Imaginary teeth can't do anything," said Elias. "They're imaginary."

Brigid shook her head vigorously. "No bites—no bites—no teeth—no teeth."

Macrina giggled. Sam picked up some pebbles and started throwing them at a nearby tree.

"I bet you're hungry, Sam," said Aunt Eva, appearing at his elbow with a plate and a napkin in her hands. "Have a sandwich."

Sam took the sandwich and sat down. Aunt Eva went back to her friends.

Elias pounded the end of his stick on the rock, like a judge calling the court to order with his gavel. "Okay, who's going to start?"

"Me!" shrieked Brigid. "Here I go!" She took a big breath. "*Once upon a time.*"

Elias, Matthew, and Macrina looked at Brigid. Brigid smiled and looked back.

"And . . . ?" Matthew waved his arms at Brigid.

"Once upon a time!" Brigid repeated. "Now it's your turn, Macrina."

Sam snickered.

"There was a nun," said Macrina, carefully not repeating the part of the story already offered by Brigid. "She was very old, and people liked her a lot."

"Abbess!" Brigid clapped her hands.

"Well, maybe," said Macrina. "You guys said you wanted the story to be at a monastery."

Elias and Matthew banged their sticks on their rocks, like applause.

"Actually," said Macrina, changing her mind, "this nun lived in a hut in the woods. She was from a family with a big farm, and they even owned the woods around their farm."

"And a beach," said Matthew. "They could be really rich. Let's make them have their own beach and five cars."

"Well, that isn't the point," said Macrina firmly. "The point is, the nun was old and she lived in the woods, and her family brought her food. She only had birds and rabbits and squirrels for company."

"Can she have mice, too?" asked Brigid. "Mice are fuzzy."

"Maybe she should have a hamster," said Macrina, pointing at Sam.

"Shut up," said Sam.

"Did your hamster come this time?" asked Elias.

"You guys, can we get back to the story?" Macrina flipped her braid over her shoulder.

Sam stood up.

"Come put your plate and napkin away," said Aunt Eva, reappearing.

"How come you keep jumping out at me?" asked Sam, wadding his paper plate and napkin into a ball. "Every time I move, *pow!* There you are."

"How about you go put that ball you just made in the trash," said Aunt Eva.

Sam started toward the edge of the picnic area.

Saucer met him at the trash can.

"Arf!" said Saucer, bouncing back and forth on the grass. He had his instructions again. *People, not sheep. Big group of people, but still, not sheep.* But Saucer couldn't help noticing that Sam kept wandering away from the group, like a stray lamb. "Arf! Arf!"

"It's trash, dog," said Sam. "It's not exciting."

"Arf!"

Sam threw his ball of trash at the can. It hit the rim and fell onto the grass.

"Arf! Arf!" Saucer pounced on it and picked it up in his mouth. He trotted over to Sam and dropped the trash on his shoe.

"Not on me, dumb dog. It goes in the can!"

Saucer stared up at Sam, waiting.

Sam turned and started to walk away.

Saucer shoved his nose under the ball of trash and flipped it into the air. It hit Sam's leg.

"Hey! Did you just throw trash at me?"

Saucer gazed pointedly at the trash can.

Sam took another step. But he looked over his shoulder, to see what Saucer would do.

Saucer jumped after him. "Arf! Arf!"

"Great. This dog is the trash police." Sam picked up the trash and walked back to the can. Saucer trotted along with him and stood nearby, watching Sam and panting eagerly.

Sam dropped the trash into the can. Saucer wagged his stumpy tail and licked Sam's shoe.

"This place is crazy," said Sam. "I just got bossed around by a dog."

Saucer threw his nose in the air and yowled.

"Can I go now?"

Saucer pawed Sam's shoe. Sam stepped back.

"Good-bye, crazy dog."

Saucer sank down on the grass and rested his nose between his paws. His tail stopped wagging.

Sam hesitated. "Well, good-bye."

Saucer's ears twitched.

Sam wandered back toward the fire.

"Hey, Elias, is it time to go yet?"

"No, it isn't," said Elias.

Macrina rolled her eyes at Sam. She could roll her eyes faster and harder than anyone else in the world. Sam rolled his eyes right back at her.

"Is there going to be a dragon in this story?" asked Matthew, ignoring them.

"Yes, and here it comes," said Macrina. "One day, a huge dragon came to the land where the nun was living. It was running around eating people and sheep and blowing fire breath on the town."

"I don't like this part!" cried Brigid, clutching Macrina's arm.

"Don't worry," said Macrina. "The dragon doesn't win."

"Now it's our turn!" shrieked the boys. "We're coming to save the nun!"

Brigid stared at them.

"I'm going to tell it," said Elias. "You act it out, Matthew."

Matthew jumped off his rock and stalked around the fire with his stick, hunting the dragon. Sam turned his back so they wouldn't think he was paying attention to their stupid story. He looked around. Grown-ups were everywhere, eating and talking. It would be hours before they went home. Sam sighed gustily.

"So then," began Elias, "the nun heard about the dragon too, and she was really freaked out! The dragon could even have started a forest fire."

Brigid squeaked.

"The nun was praying and praying," continued Elias. Matthew set his stick down for a minute and pretended to be the nun praying. He crossed himself and lay down flat on the earth, to show she was praying a whole lot.

"And just when she was praying, the dragon jumped out of the woods on one side of her hut and the biggest soldier in the neighborhood jumped out of the woods on the other side of her hut. Right in front of her!" shouted Elias.

Matthew leaped up, roaring and pawing the air. Then he ran around to the other side of Elias and leaped again, brandishing his sword.

Brigid stood up on her rock, dancing in circles. Macrina clutched the back of Brigid's dress so she wouldn't fall. Sam peeked over his shoulder for two seconds. He noticed Saucer beyond Macrina's rock, edging toward the children. Saucer's eyes followed all their movements. He looked like a person watching a tennis match. Sam snickered.

Elias gazed at his audience. He was pleased that they could tell how thrilling his story was. "The nun kept right on praying, but she was excited too because her prayers already made the soldier show up. The dragon was stomping all over the place, blowing fire at the trees. Then he turned around and saw the nun. He wanted to eat her up. It was crazy!"

Macrina stopped flipping her braid around and hung onto Brigid with both hands.

Matthew picked up Elias's stick so that he had a

stick in each hand now.

"The soldier went running right at the dragon waving two swords!" Elias waved his hand at Matthew, and Matthew charged around the rock no one was sitting on, hammering it with his two sticks.

"The nun prayed hard, and the soldier fought like crazy with his swords. No matter how much the dragon blew fire, he kept right on fighting. And then . . ." Elias paused. Brigid's eyes were round. She nearly fell off the rock.

"And then . . . the dragon turned around and started chasing the nun! Whoa! They were all running like crazy! First the nun, and she was yelling her prayers as loud as she could and hoping she didn't fall down, and then the dragon was running after her, and the soldier was running after him! It was in the woods, and they were weaving back and forth through the trees!" Elias started weaving around on his rock, over-balanced, waved his arms wildly, and jumped backwards onto the grass.

Matthew threw his two swords over the empty rock and started running around it at top speed. Saucer ran after him, barking and wagging his whole body.

"Yay!" shrieked Brigid. "Yay nun! Run fast!"

Sam stood up. "This story is stupid," he said. He brushed the grass off his pants and stomped away.

Brigid kept jumping on the rock. Elias and Matthew stood still.

"That was really mean," said Elias, his shoulders

drooping. Saucer sat down on Elias's foot and licked his leg comfortingly.

Macrina flipped her braid over her shoulder. "Don't even worry about what Sam thinks," she said. "You can ignore him. He's hopeless."

Elias glared at Macrina, more irritated with her than with Sam. "It's mean to call him hopeless."

"Well, nobody likes how he behaves," said Macrina, in her most grown-up voice.

"Nobody likes how you behave either," said Matthew, putting his arm around his brother.

"The grown-ups do," said Macrina indignantly.

"Right," said Elias. "Come on, Matthew, let's get

some more food." The two boys walked away, and Saucer trotted behind them.

Macrina shook her head and smoothed her skirt. She turned to the little girl still standing beside her on the rock. "Do you want another story, Brigid?"

"No," said Brigid. "I want my ladybug back. Where did it go?" And without further warning, Brigid burst into tears.

C H A P T E R

SIX

THE THIRD TIME Sam came to the monastery, it was midsummer. Aunt Eva filled her minivan with his cousins and their friends, but Sam kept to himself in a corner of the back seat.

When the minivan pulled into the graveled parking lot, the children clambered out, jostling each other cheerfully and ignoring grumpy Sam. Sam scuffed the toe of his shoe on the gravel and put his hands in his pockets.

"Here we go, Sam." Aunt Eva handed him a

two-pound bag of rice. "You can help me carry this." She looked around at the group of children. "Does everyone have something? Is there anything left in the van?"

"We have everything," said Macrina, sticking her head back into the van to check.

"Let's go," said Elias.

"My mother made me come here," muttered Sam, scowling at the rice.

"That's right," said Aunt Eva. "She's smarter than you think."

"Could I wait in the van?"

"We need you to stay with the family, Sam. We aren't going to leave you here alone in the parking lot all day."

Sam poked the bag of rice with his finger.

"Try not to break it, Sam. It would be a shame to waste food the sisters could eat."

Sam's cousins and their friends ran to greet Sister Katherine and Sister Anna, who were waiting for them at the gate. Sam trudged behind them, kicking gravel on purpose with every step.

Suddenly, Saucer bounced out from behind Sister Katherine and flung himself down on the grass at the edge of the parking lot. He rolled onto his back and wiggled as hard as he could, flopping from side to side and waving his legs in the air, arching his neck to rub his pointy ears backward onto the grass. His tongue hung out of his mouth sideways. He barked.

Sam stopped in his tracks.

"Hey, trash-police dog. You remember me?"

"That's Saucer," Sister Katherine told him, smiling. Saucer flipped over onto his legs again and bounced back and forth on the grass, barking at Sam, urging him to come right over and say hello.

Sam came over. Saucer barked. Sam set down his bag of rice and patted Saucer. Saucer licked his hand and then turned to Sister Katherine.

"Saucer says we should go in now," said Sister Katherine, smiling. "Look how he's watching all of you. He's wishing you were sheep!"

"Baaaaaaaaaaaaa!" bleated Elias.

"Don't do that," said Macrina. "You'll make him think we're all sheep."

"That would make him happy!" Elias grinned at Saucer. "Baaaaaa!"

"It will make him bite our ankles!" Macrina stepped back a pace.

"I hope he bites yours first," muttered Sam.

All the children wanted to pat Saucer. Saucer frisked and barked and licked all the hands he could reach. But when, after a minute or two, Sister Katherine led the children through the gate into the monastery, Saucer went back to Sam and nudged his leg.

Sam looked down at Saucer. "Okay, dog," he said. "Now what?"

Saucer trotted forward. Then he trotted back to Sam, nipped his shoelaces, and trotted forward again. Sam started walking. Saucer jumped on Sam's feet.

"What? You said to walk!"

Saucer trotted back to the bag of rice Sam had abandoned on the ground.

"Oh, all right." Sam came back and picked it up.

"Arf!" said Saucer. He bounced across the grass and through the monastery gate, and Sam followed him.

Inside the gate, the children crowded around Sister Katherine and Sister Anna. Saucer sat on his haunches and pointed his ears forward at the nuns.

"Listen," said Aunt Eva, raising her eyebrows. The children stopped talking. The eyebrows always made them stop.

Aunt Eva smiled. "The sisters are going to tell us about our day."

"Arf!" said Saucer. Everybody laughed.

"Can I put this rice down?" asked Sam, loudly.

"I need you to hold that rice, Sam," said Aunt Eva.

"We can take it to the kitchen in just a minute," said Sister Anna.

Sam started kicking the gravel. Saucer trotted over and sat down on Sam's foot.

"Some of you will come with me to the church, and some of you will go with Sister Anna to the kitchen," Sister Katherine explained. "Aunt Eva will take a few of you over to the prayer garden."

Sam's friends and cousins started raising their hands, asking to go to the kitchen, or the garden, or the church. Sam thought about putting down the rice again, but Aunt Eva and Saucer both had their eyes on him now.

Sam sighed.

Saucer nuzzled his leg and took a little bite of his shoe lace.

"Crazy dog," muttered Sam.

"Arf!" said Saucer, and grinned at him.

"You're in my group, Sam," said Sister Katherine. "We're going up to the church. You can give your rice to Sister Anna now."

"Thank you, Sam," said Sister Anna, holding out her hands.

"Welcome," mumbled Sam. His face felt hot.

"Saucer, let Sam walk," said Sister Katherine. Saucer hopped off Sam's foot and scampered in circles in the grass.

"But I don't want to go to church," said Sam, staying where he was.

Sister Katherine didn't turn around. She had three other children with her, and they were already moving up the path.

"Maybe I just won't come," said Sam, a little louder, and at that moment, Saucer took a large mouthful of Sam's left pant leg and began to pull him up the path.

"Hey!" shouted Sam. "Your crazy dog is eating my pants!"

Sister Katherine laughed. It was a happy sound. "He wants you to come to church! Saucer loves to go to church. Wait and see."

"I'm coming," said Sam, "but only because my pants are coming."

"Why don't you want to come to church, Sam?" asked Sister Katherine, turning and walking backward so she could see his face.

"There's nothing interesting at church," said Sam, hopping along with Saucer hanging off his leg.

"Did you know we have dead men's bones at church?" asked Sister Katherine.

"What?!?"

"We do. In a special silver chest."

"Real bones from dead guys?"

"Come and see."

"Okay," said Sam, and Saucer let go of his pant leg and galloped up the path on his short legs, barking and wagging his stumpy tail.

"Crazy dog," muttered Sam. "Now my pants have dog slobber on them."

But he kept walking.

When Sam reached the church, the others had already gone inside, but Saucer was waiting for him at the door.

"Are you going to church, crazy dog?" asked Sam.

Saucer pranced over the threshold and stopped

just inside the church. He put his head down and licked the floor, just once, like a kiss.

"This place is crazy," said Sam to himself. "The dog goes to church, and they have dead-guy bones. I'm going in there. I bet I never saw anything like this."

Sam stepped over the threshold and stood next to Saucer, who was sitting quietly on the smooth stone floor.

Sam saw golden-brown candles standing in a box full of sand. The candlelight flickered, and he saw patient, solemn faces with dark eyes, watching him from the gilded icons on the walls. He sniffed the air and noticed its soft, spicy fragrance as he breathed in and out. He heard Sister Katherine's gentle voice and saw his friends standing by a wooden table along the wall inside

the sanctuary. He saw more candles, more icons, and a little metal basket hanging from golden chains with bells on them.

Sister Katherine beckoned.

Sam walked carefully across the floor. He felt like a person climbing a mountain, looking for safe places to put his feet down, looking for something strong to hold onto with his hands.

"This is our reliquary," whispered Sister Katherine, holding out a small silver case. "Open it."

Sam used the tips of his fingers to lift the lid.

"Those little openings each hold a fragment of bone. Do you see them?"

Sam stared. "From real dead guys?"

"Not just real. Real and special. Those are the bones of saints."

Sam leaned closer. "Does it smell weird?"

"That's myrrh. It's what holiness smells like."

Sam held out one finger. Sister Katherine smiled and nodded at him. Sam let his finger come to rest on a small smooth piece of glass. Under it was a bone fragment from a saint. He let his finger rest there for one second, then another. Then he backed away.

When he got to the door, Saucer was there waiting for him.

"I'm going outside," said Sam. Saucer followed him and plopped down on the grass. Sam knelt down next to him and scratched the fuzzy space between Saucer's pointy ears.

Saucer settled further into the grass. His front legs stuck out in front of him. His back legs stuck out behind him.

"You look like Super Dog," said Sam. "You just need a cape."

Saucer rolled on his back and waved his legs in the air.

"Now you look like crazy dog again."

Saucer barked.

When it was time to go home, Sam lagged behind the other children and the nuns on the way back to the parking lot. The children were all talking to each other, and Aunt Eva was talking to the nuns. Sam was talking to Saucer.

"I saw some dead guys' bones, crazy dog."

"Arf!"

"It was weird and cool."

"Arf!"

"I don't know about this place."

"Arf! Arf!"

"Crazy dog."

Aunt Eva turned when she reached the monastery gate and waited for Sam to catch up. "I see you made a friend, Sam."

"This dog is crazy."

"Are you sure about that?"

Sam scuffed his toe on the ground. Saucer licked his shoe.

"This dog bit my pants and dragged me to church," said Sam.

Aunt Eva reached down and patted Saucer on the head. "Good dog, Saucer," she said. "You do whatever it takes."

CHAPTER

SEVEN

THE NEXT MORNING, Saucer woke early. The air felt warm and still. He could hear the silence around him, where yesterday the air rang with children's voices. It was the hot dry season when Sister Katherine left extra water dishes in the animal pens. The grass browned and crinkled up under the sun.

Saucer marched around the pens for a few minutes. He lapped his water and flopped onto the dirt, resting his nose on his front paws. He imagined hundreds of sheep scattering over a rocky hillside. In his mind's eye, he chased them down and brought them together. The sheep marched in rows. They bleated in harmony, singing a happy sheep song. Saucer sighed contentedly.

Saucer's dream vanished. Something was wrong.

Saucer's nose told him first. He smelled something unfamiliar. He gathered his short legs under him and stood up. He lifted his head, ears twitching.

Bethlehem saw Saucer. His long gray ears flicked around, first one way, then the other. He brayed. Dickens the duck made a motion, and Shakespeare started rounding up the other ducks without waiting for Charlotte and Emily to second it. The goats bunched together. The two bunnies, Mary and Martha, hopped in circles. Aero and Butterscotch abandoned their corners and came to the fence, a few feet away from Saucer.

Saucer smelled smoke. He raced to the end of the row of pens, and there, he saw it. Flames flickered in the undergrowth at the edge of the woods behind the farm. The fire was still small, but the grass and scrub were dry. The fire would not be small for long.

"Arf! Arf! Arf!!" Saucer barked urgently. Sister Katherine was at morning prayers with the other nuns, in the church on the little hill to the west. The fire wasn't large enough yet to roar and snap. The smoke hung close in the still air. The nuns might not notice the fire until it burned out of control.

Saucer barked again, but now he wasn't frightened. Saucer knew what to do.

"Arf! Arf, arf, arf!"

Saucer galloped up and down between the pens,

barking and waving his nose, wide-eyed and fierce. The animals stopped milling around. They were frightened, but they could see that Saucer was not.

Listen! said Saucer's bark.

The animals listened.

I can help. Watch me and follow!

The animals stood still and watched.

When he had everyone's attention, Saucer marched to the first pen. Aero and Butterscotch were there, and Saucer knew Aero could help him.

Saucer bounced up against the gate to Aero's pen, stretching his nose to reach the latch and pop it up. Aero started to scramble over the top of the fence, then hopped down again, unwilling to leave Butterscotch.

Saucer tried twice to reach the latch. It took his biggest bounce to get his pointed nose high enough. The third time, his nose banged against the latch (*Ouch!* "Arf!") and knocked it over. Aero jumped against the gate from the inside. He dashed out, with Butterscotch waddling behind him.

Together, Saucer and Aero pushed open the squeaky gate and raced out of the animal farm. Butterscotch waddled behind, squawking directions to them, trying to keep up. Past the apple orchard they went, past the gardens, to the place where the path wound up a gentle hill to the church door. Saucer streaked up the path and jumped against the door, barking as loudly as he could. Aero ran in circles on the path behind him, and their barks alternated like a sound and its echo.

"Arf! Woof! Arf! Woof!"

The church doors burst open and nuns streamed out onto the path. Saucer ran one way, and Aero ran the other way, circling the nuns, nipping at their ankles, urging them to come.

Sister Katherine looked down the path toward the animal farm. She saw black smoke billowing up from the woods behind.

"Call the fire department, Sister Anna," she shouted over her shoulder, and began to run down the path.

"Arf!" Saucer barked encouragingly and plunged after her. Aero ran zig-zags behind them, looking for Butterscotch, who had stopped to rest along the way. He shortened his stride when he found her, and he led her back to the pens. Butterscotch clucked and squeaked all the way.

When the rescue party reached the animal farm, Sister Katherine charged through the gate, with Saucer right on her heels. She ran along the line of pens, opening doors and lifting latches.

"Now, Saucer! Now is the time to lead!"

The ducks and goats came out as soon as their pens were open, and Bethlehem happily followed the goats, but Mary and Martha were too surprised to move. Butterscotch hopped into their pen, squawking loudly, and pecked at them once or twice, cocking her head to the door. *Come along, bunnies. You can't stay here. I don't want to peck you, but I will if you don't start hopping.*

Mary and Martha followed Butterscotch. They hopped so close behind her that Butterscotch had to speed up to avoid being knocked over. Butterscotch clucked and shook her feathered head.

Dry branches on the ground caught fire, and the edges of the grass by the woods began to smoke. The flames spread.

Saucer barked again, running around the milling group of animals. At first, Saucer's herd was confused. The ducks bumped into the prancing goats. The bunnies knocked Butterscotch over. Bethlehem trotted in circles, braying distractedly. Sister Katherine waved her hands at them, trying to calm them and urge them on all with one motion. The animals stared at her for a few seconds, then went back to milling around.

Saucer wasn't discouraged. He had been waiting for this moment all his short life, and he knew what to do.

Saucer raced around the group, first one way, then the other, nipping at goat ankles, nudging ducklings. Aero copied him. Saucer went one way, Aero went the other way. The animals calmed down and came together. They were a herd now, and Saucer was their leader.

Barking instructions, Saucer led his herd along the path. Aero brought up the rear with Sister Katherine, helping Saucer keep the group together. Each time a duckling waddled off or a goat sprang into the bushes, Saucer bounded over to return the straying one to the herd.

Along the path they went, past the apple orchard and the gardens, to the place where the path wound up the hill to the church door. The door opened, and the abbess came out onto the path, holding the arm of a

young nun who had stayed to pray with her while the others helped the firefighters.

Seeing the abbess and her nun, the animals sighed with relief and began to explain what happened, all at once, at the tops of their voices.

"Baaaa! Quack! Hee-haw! Buk-buk! Woof! Arf!"

Bethlehem brayed and pointed back to the farm and the fire with his soft gray nose. Mary and Martha snuggled up to Butterscotch. Butterscotch fell over and squawked. The goats Hop, Skip, Jump, Et Cetera, and So Forth scampered up to the church doors to see if there were more interesting nuns inside. Dickens, Shakespeare, Emily, Jane, Cuthbert, Ignatius, Kassiani, Photios, Moses, and Daniel quacked and waddled round and round. Aero chased after them. He wished they would stop running in circles.

Saucer kept the animals together all morning. He settled them in the shady grass beside the church. They were only a few steps from the path, and the wall behind them helped Saucer and Aero keep the herd together. Saucer knew Sister Katherine would take them back to their homes as soon as she could.

The nuns helped the firefighters put out the fire. It was a long, hot day, and when it was over, their faces and hands were scorched and sooty, and they were tired to the bone.

The air smelled smoky and bitter. One end of the nuns' quarters was damaged, and the little bookstore had burned to the ground, but without Saucer's warning, the fire would have spread farther, and the whole monastery might have been lost.

The nuns made a feast for the firefighters to

thank them before they returned to the fire station. But first, Sister Katherine told the animals it was safe for them to go home. Saucer, Aero, and Butterscotch were still standing watch while the others rested in the shady grass.

Sister Katherine let Saucer lead his herd back to their pens. She brushed his fur, refilled his water dish, and gave him a cookie. Saucer flopped down next to his doghouse and stretched his short legs. His nose sank drowsily onto his front paws.

Saucer fell asleep.

Sister Katherine stooped to lay her hand on Saucer's head. "Bless you, little faithful one," she whispered. "God knew better than we did what you were meant for, and when He called you, you were listening."

EPILOGUE

"SAUCER."

Saucer's eyes drifted open.

"Saucer. Are you awake?"

Saucer's head came up. He looked around.

"Over here, crazy dog." The latch squeaked. "I'm coming in."

Sam sat down cross-legged on the ground beside Saucer. "Aunt Eva drove me here because we heard about the fire. You were on the news. The TV man said a dog told the nuns the woods were on fire."

Saucer sniffed Sam's leg.

"It was you, wasn't it?"

Saucer sat up on his haunches and barked.

Sam grinned. "I knew it." He stuffed his hand into the pocket of his shorts and pulled out a wadded paper napkin. He unfolded it. Inside, Saucer saw a curly, crispy strip of bacon. His tongue rolled out of his mouth. He scooched closer to Sam.

"Here, crazy dog. I brought you this because you're smart." Sam held out his hand and Saucer snatched up the bacon. He chewed quickly. His stumpy tail wagged against the dusty ground.

Sam looked around. "The farm's okay, but that

building over there looks pretty burnt."

Saucer sighed gustily and licked his chops.

"I don't have any more bacon. But I could bring you some another time."

Saucer stretched his front paws and wiggled. He settled on the ground and rested his head on Sam's lap. Sam scratched the soft fur between Saucer's ears.

"Okay," said Sam. "I'll bring you another treat, next time I come."

MELINDA JOHNSON is an Orthodox Christian, wife, mother, and writer. She has a Master's in English Literature because she loved literature classes so much she couldn't stop taking them. When she is not seeing "heaven in a wildflower," Melinda enjoys writing for children, walking and talking, and befriending small furry creatures.

Also by Melinda Johnson

The Barn and the Book

Sam wants to know if animals (especially Saucer!) can speak at midnight on Christmas Eve. Grace and Macrina are competing to write a story, and Elias is losing his patience. Meanwhile, Sister Anna hopes God will rescue her from teaching Sunday school. Christmas is coming, but hearts are full of secrets and frustrations. *The Barn and the Book* is a story about the traps we build when we try to see in the dark. We tumble into trouble and confusion on our own, but God can steer us clear of our traps and shine His kindly light into our darkness.

ISBN: 978-1-944967-43-7

https://store.ancientfaith.com/
the-barn-and-the-book/

READINGS FROM UNDER THE GRAPEVINE

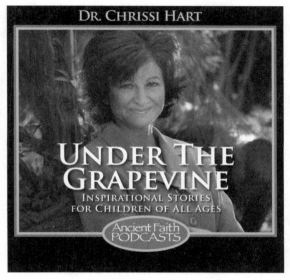

Enjoy readings by Dr. Chrissi Hart of inspirational stories for children of all ages. This podcast concentrates on Orthodox Christian books and other classic literature from a variety of sources.

http://www.ancientfaith.com/podcasts/grapevine

Special Agents of Christ
A Prayer Book for Young Orthodox Saints
by Annalisa Boyd

You're never too young to be one of God's "special agents"—the people He uses to accomplish His will in the world. In this prayer book written especially for middle-grade children, the author of the popular teen prayer book *Hear Me* uses the examples of special agents of the past—the saints—to encourage children to serve God here and now. In addition to morning and evening prayers, prayers for special needs, and psalms to pray, Special Agents of Christ includes "training drills" on preparing for confession, understanding the Liturgy and the clergy's vestments, and more.

• Paperback, 96 pages, ISBN 978-1-936270-55-2

Bearing the Saint
by Donna Farley

Edmund is just an ordinary fisherman's son from the island of Lindisfarne whose one great talent and joy is running as a messenger for his bishop. But when Viking invaders threaten the holy island and its great treasure, the relics of St. Cuthbert, Edmund's life changes forever. Along with his whole village, he must accompany their beloved saint on a perilous pilgrimage that will carry him across England, through adventure, heartbreak, miraculous deliverance, and budding love, all the way to manhood.

Bearing the Saint brings to life the late ninth century in

Northumbria, a turbulent period of invasion and conquest that concluded with an uneasy peace between Saxon and Dane. This gripping story, infused with the holy breath of St. Cuthbert, will hold readers of all ages spellbound.

A chapter book for ages 10 and up.

• Paperback, 265 pages, ISBN 978-1-936270-04-0

Keeper of the Light
St. Macrina the Elder, Grandmother of Saints

by Bev. Cooke, illustrated by Bonnie Gillis

The road to sainthood takes a lifetime to travel. . . . Late in the fourth century, Christians are labeled enemies of the Roman Empire—hounded, arrested, tortured, and executed. Macrina and her husband Basil, once-wealthy Christians, flee with their small son to the mountainous forests south of the Black Sea. So begins Macrina's adventure in faith, as she undertakes the process of becoming one of the most influential women in sacred history, the mother and grandmother of saints. She is truly a great confessor of the Orthodox Christian faith. A chapter book with black-and-white illustrations.

A chapter book for ages 12 and up.

• Paperback, 200 pages, ISBN 978-1-888212-77-8

A Child's Guide to the Divine Liturgy

Compiled and edited by Ancient Faith Publishing, illustrated by Megan Gilbert

This wonderful tool for Orthodox children is designed as an aid to help them negotiate their way through the Divine Liturgy and learn more about the Church and our faith.

Small and easy to hold, with engaging illustrations, the guide is divided into six color-coded sections: Preparing for the Divine Liturgy; The Divine Liturgy; Salt and Light; The 12 Feasts; Words to Know; and Glossary.

This guide is written to appeal to children ages 2–10. The very young child will learn basic vocabulary and come to recognize the various milestones in the Divine Liturgy. For the older child, several longer psalms, quotes, and prayers are included; plus the 12 feast icons and kontakia; and an extensive glossary filled with terms and vocabulary often heard throughout the liturgical year.

• Paperback, 112 pages, 4.75 X 6 inches, ISBN 978-1-936270-17-0

A Gift for Matthew

by Nick Muzekari, illustrated by Masha Lobastov

Matthew's excited to visit a monastery. A monk there is teaching him to paint icons! Matthew learns about sketching images, mixing pigments, and painting all the layers of the sacred images. And when he gets home, he finds a surprise gift just for him.

A children's picture book.

• Hardcover, 32 pages, 8 X 10 inches, ISBN 978-1-936270-92-7

Lucia, Saint of Light

by Katherine Bolger Hyde, illustrated by Daria Fisher

Long revered in both East and West, St. Lucia is an early virgin martyr whose life and legacy shine as a light of faith, hope, and compassion in the darkness of winter and sin. *Lucia, Saint of Light* introduces young readers to both her life and her delightful festival as it is traditionally celebrated in Sweden and around the world.

Daria Fisher's warm and vivid illustrations will make this book a favorite with children and parents alike.

A children's picture book.

• Hardcover, 32 pages, 8 X 10 inches, ISBN 978-0-9822770-4-1

The Miracle of the Red Egg

by Elizabeth Crispina Johnson, illustrated by Daria Fisher

At Pascha, Orthodox all over the world dye and bless red eggs. Here is the story of how this tradition started—way back in apostolic times, with St. Mary Magdalene and a blessed miracle that dazzled the unbelieving Roman emperor with the reality and power of Christ's Resurrection.

A children's picture book.

• Hardcover, 32 pages, 8 X 10 inches, ISBN 978-1-936270-59-0

Sweet Song
A Story of Saint Romanos the Melodist

by Jane G. Meyer, illustrated by Dorrie Papademetriou

Young Romanos is devoted to Christ and His Mother and longs to be able to sing his praises to them. But when he tries, his voice croaks, and the words won't come. The other cantors make fun of him—until one miraculous Christmas Eve.

A children's picture book.

• Hardcover, 32 pages, 8 X 10 inches, ISBN 978-1-936270-43-9

The Hidden Garden
A Story of the Heart

by Jane G. Meyer, illustrated by Masha Lobastov

Within every heart is a hidden garden. We can neglect it until the weeds take over and the flowers wither and die. Or, with the help of Christ, we can care for it and make it a place of beauty, grace, and joy. This charming parable will encourage children (and adults) to open the gate to Christ and tend the garden of their heart with loving care.

A children's picture book.

• Hardcover, 32 pages, 8 X 10 inches, ISBN 978-1-936270-38-5

And Then Nicholas Sang
The Story of the Trisagion Hymn

by Elizabeth Johnson, illustrated by Masha Lobastov

Nicholas the Chatterer was an ordinary young boy who loved his home in Constantinople almost as much as he loved to talk. That is, until the day the angels caught him up out of an earthquake and taught him to sing. Then he became Nicholas the Singer. His song saved the city from the earthquakes and entered into the Church's liturgy for all ages, as the Trisagion Hymn. The lyrical text and vivid illustrations show children that they too can be used by God to bring blessings to all mankind.

• Hardcover, 32 pages, 8 X 10 inches, ISBN 978-1-936270-05-7

For complete ordering information, see store.ancientfaith.com or call customer service at 800-967-7377.

Ancient Faith Publishing hopes you have enjoyed and benefited from this book. The proceeds from the sales of our books only partially cover the costs of operating our nonprofit ministry—which includes both the work of **Ancient Faith Publishing** and the work of **Ancient Faith Radio.** Your financial support makes it possible to continue this ministry both in print and online. Donations are tax-deductible and can be made at www.ancient-faith.com.

To view our other publications,
log onto our website: **store.ancientfaith.com**

 **ANCIENT FAITH RADIO**

Bringing you Orthodox Christian music, readings,
prayers, teaching, and podcasts 24 hours a day since 2004 at
www.ancientfaith.com